I0669678

Oliver Herford, Press Heintzemann

An Alphabet of Celebrities

Oliver Herford, Press Heintzemann

An Alphabet of Celebrities

ISBN/EAN: 9783337085315

Printed in Europe, USA, Canada, Australia, Japan

Cover: Foto ©Andreas Hilbeck / pixelio.de

More available books at **www.hansebooks.com**

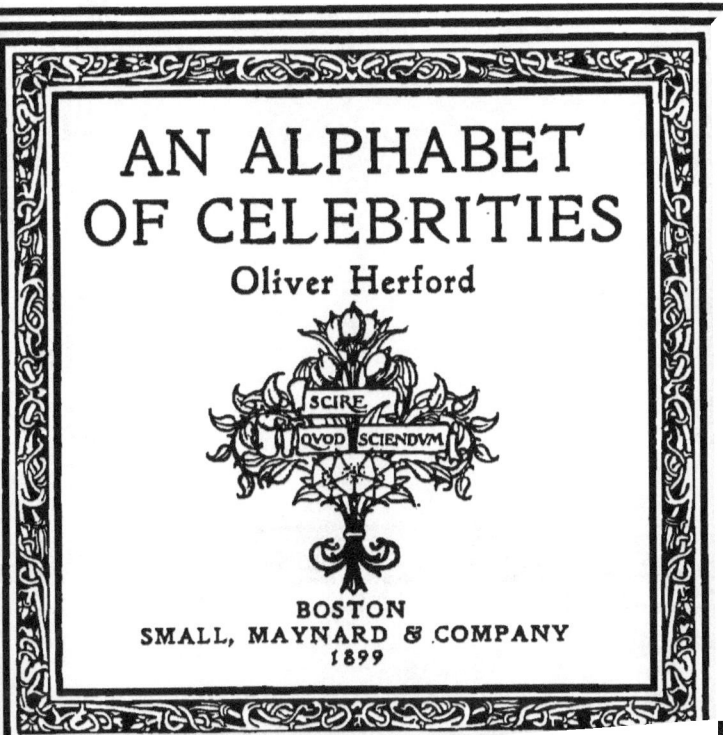

AN ALPHABET OF CELEBRITIES

Oliver Herford

SCIRE QVOD SCIENDVM

BOSTON
SMALL, MAYNARD & COMPANY
1899

An Alphabet of Celebrities

A'S Albert Edward,
  well meaning but
  flighty,
Who invited King Arthur,
  the blameless and
  mighty,
To meet Alcibiades and
  Aphrodite.

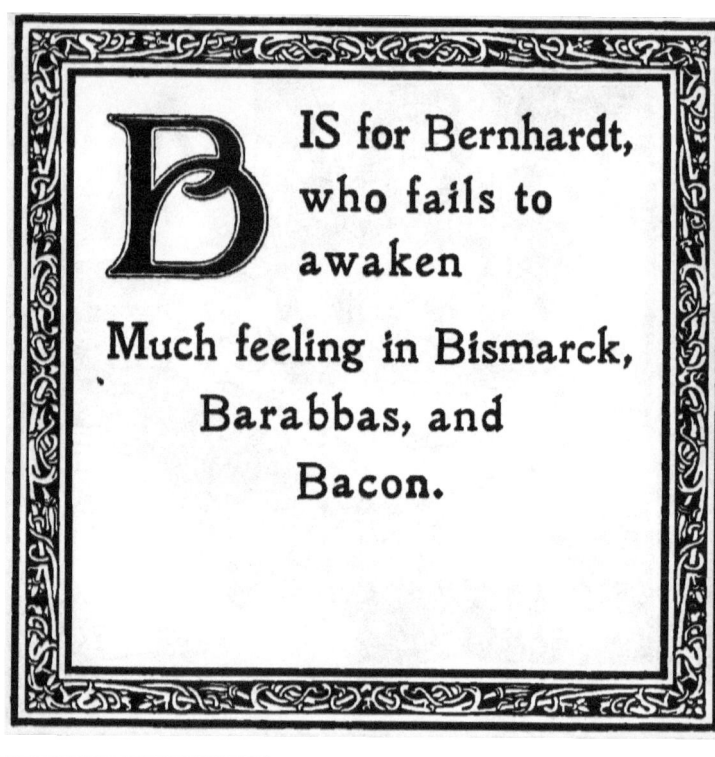

B IS for Bernhardt, who fails to awaken

Much feeling in Bismarck, Barabbas, and Bacon.

C IS Columbus, who tries
to explain
How to balance an egg —
to the utter disdain
Of Confucius, Carlyle,
Cleopatra, and Cain.

D'S for Diogenes,
Darwin,
and Dante,
Who delight in the dance
Of a Darling
Bacchante.

E IS for Edison, making believe
He's invented a clever contrivance for Eve,
Who complained that she never could laugh in her sleeve.

F IS for Franklin,
who fearfully
shocks

The feelings of Fenelon,
Faber, and Fox.

G IS Godiva, whose great bareback feat
She kindly but firmly declines to repeat,
Though Gounod and Goldsmith implore and entreat.

H IS for Handel,
who pours
out his soul
Through the bagpipes to
Howells and Homer,
who roll
On the floor in an ecstasy
past all control.

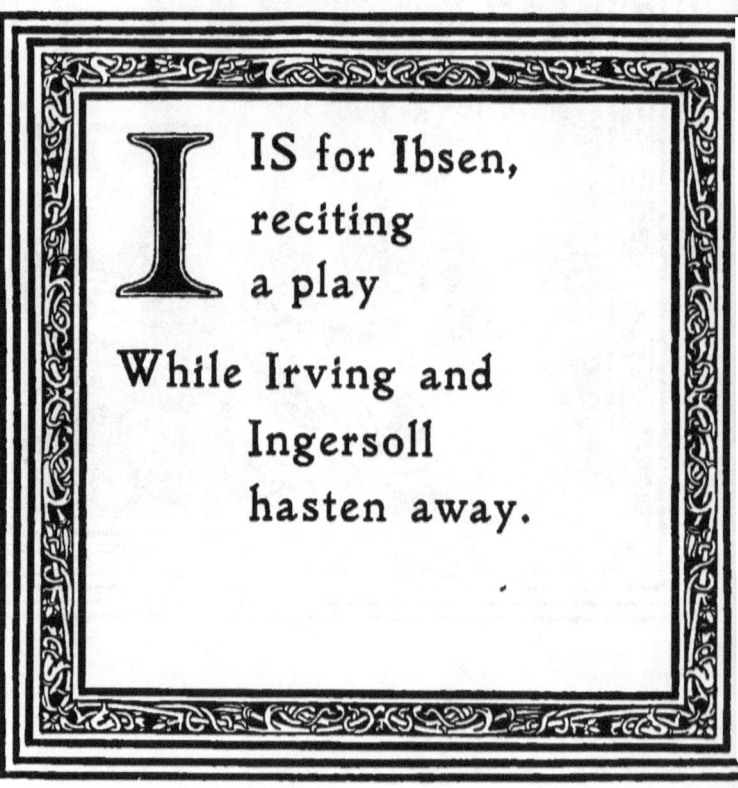

I IS for Ibsen, reciting a play

While Irving and Ingersoll hasten away.

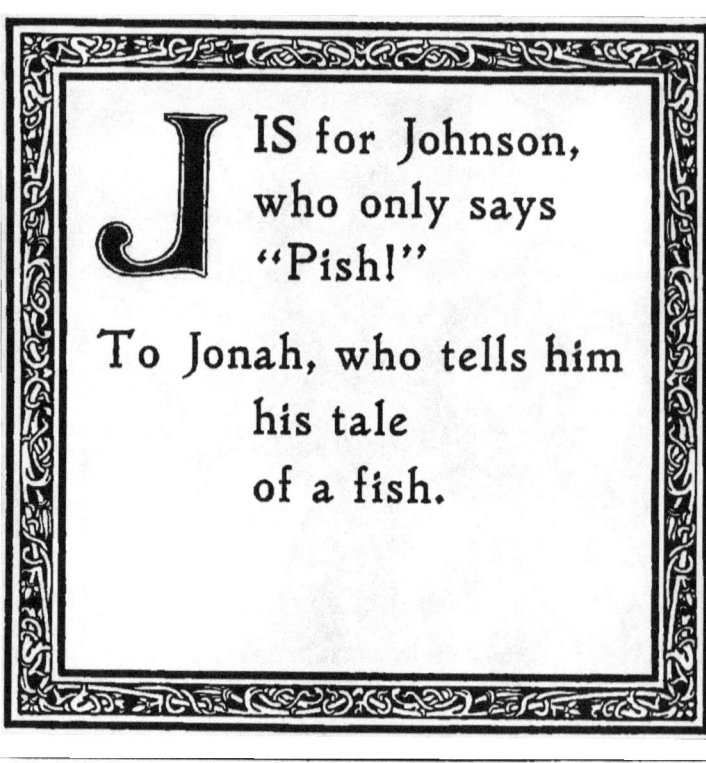

J IS for Johnson,
who only says
"Pish!"
To Jonah, who tells him
his tale
of a fish.

K IS the Kaiser, who kindly repeats

Some original verses to Kipling and Keats.

L IS Lafontaine,
who finds he's
unable

To interest Luther and
Liszt in his fable,

While Loie continues
to dance on the table.

M IS Macduff,
who's prevailed
upon Milton

And Montaigne and
Manon to each try
a kilt on.

N IS Napoleon, shrouded
in gloom,
With Nero, Narcissus,
and Nordau, to whom
He's explaining the
manual of arms with
a broom.

O IS for Oliver, casting aspersion

On Omar, that awfully dissolute Persian,

Though secretly longing to join the diversion.

P IS for Peter, who hollers "No! No!"
Through the keyhole to Paine, Paderewski, and Poe.

Q IS the Queen, so noble and free—

For further particulars look under V.

R'S Rubenstein, playing that old thing in F

To Rollo and Rembrandt, who wish they were deaf.

S IS for Swinburne, who, seeking the true, the good, and the beautiful, visits the Zoo,
Where he chances on Sappho and Mr. Sardou,
And Socrates, all with the same end in view.

T IS for Talleyrand toasting
Miss Truth,
By the side of her well,
in a glass of vermouth,
And presenting Mark
Twain as the friend
of his youth.

U IS for Undine, pursuing Ulysses

And Umberto, who flee her damp, death-dealing kisses.

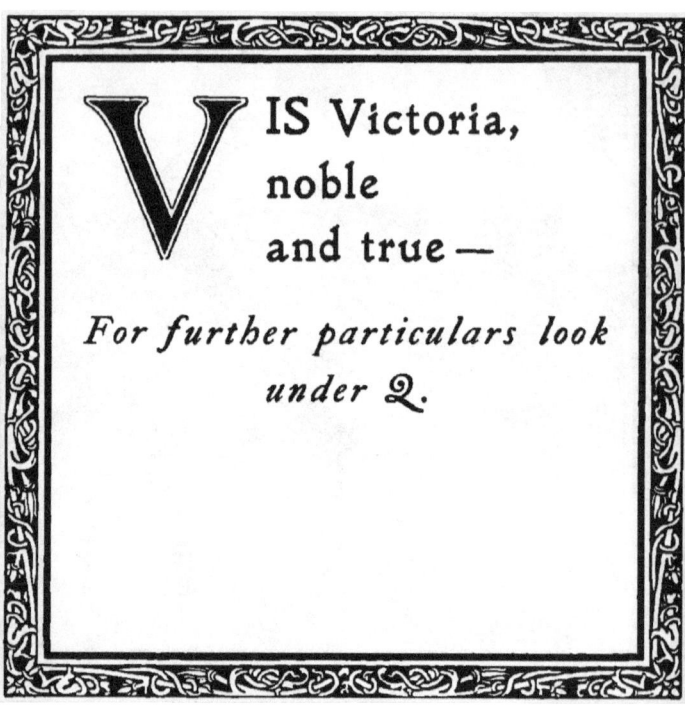

V IS Victoria,
noble
and true —

*For further particulars look
under Q.*

W'S Wagner, who sang and played lots for Washington, Wesley, and good Doctor Watts. His prurient plots pained Wesley and Watts, But Washington said he "enjoyed them in spots."

X IS Xantippe, who's having her say,

And frightening the army of Xerxes away.

Y IS for Young, the great Mormon saint,

Who thinks little Yum Yum and Yvette so quaint,

He has to be instantly held in restraint.

Z IS for Zola, presenting *La Terre*

To Zenobia the brave and Zuleika the fair,

Whose blushes they artfully conceal with their hair.

This Alphabet of Celebrities written & pictured by Oliver Herford with a border & initial letters by Bertram Grosvenor Goodhue and end papers & cover design by E. B. Bird is printed for Small Maynard & Company at the Heintzemann Press in Boston U. S. A. in the month of November MDCCCXCIX